THE BIG BANG
THEORY

THE BIG BANG THEORY

Based on the television
episode *The Big Bang Theory*,
written by Scott Guy

Adapted by Gerry Bailey

Illustrations by Henryk Szor

SCHOLASTIC INC.

New York   Toronto   London   Auckland   Sydney
Mexico City   New Delhi   Hong Kong   Buenos Aires

ISBN 0-439-37023-X

Produced by Scholastic Inc. in 2001 under license from Just Licensing Ltd.
© 2000 Just Entertainment Ltd
Mike Young Productions Inc
Digital Content Development Corporation Ltd.

12 11 10 9 8 7 6 5 4 3   1 2 3 4 5 6/0

Printed in the U.S.A.
First Scholastic printing, November 2001

THE BIG BANG THEORY

THE BUTT-UGLY MARTIANS' THEME SONG

B.K.M! B.K.M! B.K.M! (ah ha!) B.K.M!
We are the Martians,
The Butt-Ugly Martians.
We are the Martians,
The Butt-Ugly Martians.

We don't really want a war.
I just want to hoverboard.
We don't want to conquer Earth.
I just want to fill my girth.

We are the Martians,
The Butt-Ugly Martians.
We are the Martians,
The Butt-Ugly Martians.

If you try to go too far,
You will see how tough we are.
If you try it any way,
Then you're gonna hear me say.

B.K.M! (oh yeah!) B.B.K.M! (Let's get ugly!)
B.K.M! B.B.K.M!
We are the Martians,
The Butt-Ugly Martians.
We are the Martians,
The Butt-Ugly Martians.

THE STORY SO FAR...

THE YEAR IS 2053 and the Martians have landed on Earth! The advance troops — Commander B.Bop-A-Luna, Tech Commando 2-T-Fru-T, and Corporal Do-Wah Diddy — have been sent to Earth by their ruthless leader, Emperor Bog, to take over the planet.

Back on board the *Bogstar* spaceship, Emperor Bog along with his sidekick, the evil Dr. Damage, is waiting for his advance troops to complete the first phase of the invasion. But the three Butt-Ugly Martians love Earth so much, they have no intention of taking it over!

Instead, they hang out with their Earthling friends, Mike, Angela, and Cedric, watching TV, eating fast food, avoiding Stoat Muldoon — Earth's number one alien hunter (or so he thinks!) and generally enjoying themselves.

To convince Emperor Bog that the invasion is progressing well, they regularly send him fake battle reports. Meanwhile, with the help of their incredibly useful robotic canine, Dog, the Butt-Uglies are actually Earth's heroes, protecting the planet from alien attack!

B! K! M!

Sent to conquer planet Earth,
Our mission is now to protect it.
Courage to fight for freedom.
Wisdom to use these powers for
the good of mankind.
Power to defend against all invaders.

MULDOON GETS LUCKY

THE THREE BUTT-UGLY Martians, B.Bop, 2-T, and Do-Wah, stood on a cylindrical platform, lit by flickering stars. They were wearing transparent space helmets. Their Earthling friends, Angela and Cedric, stood on another cylindrical platform. Suddenly a razor-sharp pyramid-shaped shard shot through space and headed for the Martians. It was about to impale them! They ducked in the nick of time.

The shard then headed straight for Angela and Cedric. The kids jumped and the shard passed harmlessly beneath them before heading back toward the Butt-Uglies.

The Martians took their cue from the kids and jumped, too. All, that is, except Do-Wah, who did the opposite and flattened himself against the platform. The shard whizzed underneath B.Bop and 2-T as they jumped, and passed over Do-Wah. Unfortunately for Do-Wah, B.Bop then landed on him with a splat!

But the worst was not over yet. Angela pointed nervously to the horizon and the Butt-Uglies turned to look. Six more pyramid-shaped shards were heading straight for the platforms!

Do-Wah reached for his wrist gauntlet

and fired a laser beam at the oncoming shards. However, from his position beneath B.Bop, his aim was less accurate than normal. His shot blazed off target.

Then everyone heard an ominous electronic spluttering as the starry background and pyramid shards vanished.

Everything went quiet and lights flickered on, illuminating the scene. It was the Butt-Uglies' hideout on Earth, the old arcade, ZAPZ. The Martians and kids had been playing a virtual reality game.

The Butt-Uglies, Angela, and Cedric stood in front of a blue screen and looked at the projector that had created the background. Now it sparked and hissed as its life ebbed away. All eyes turned toward the unfortunate Do-Wah.

"Hey, some fancy shooting there, Roy Rogers," said 2-T sarcastically as he stepped off the virtual reality platform.

"Yeah," said B.Bop, "that's the second projector you've shot out in two days!"

"I'm sorry," said Do-Wah. "It's just, I get excited. I love virtual games."

4

"So do we — so do you mind not des-
troying them!" said Cedric as he and
Angela stepped off their platform.

"Can you fix it, 2-T?" asked Angela.

2-T walked over to the blasted
projector, fanned away some smoke and

laughed in disbelief. "I'm sorry," he said. "I thought you asked me if I could fix it! Come on! You're talking to 2-T, here, Guru of Gadgets…Master of the Mechanical… Dean of Devices…"

"She asked you a simple question," interrupted B.Bop.

2-T looked deflated. "I dunno. He fried it pretty good."

Cedric looked at his watch. "Hey, I thought Mike was gonna join us," he said.

"Nah, he can't," said Angela. "He left his biology report to the very last minute, as always. So he's being a good boy and quietly working at home."

But, unknown to Angela, Mike was nowhere near his home, or his homework. Instead, he was at the hoverboard park, hitting a

720° tuck-spin and having the time of his life. "Yeeeee haaaah!" he yelled as he landed on the bottom of the ramp. It was a perfect stunt, but now it was time to go.

Mike headed out of the park. He stopped just outside the gates. "Dog, you done?" he asked the robotic canine, who was hidden behind a tree.

Dog nodded and barked.

"Great! Thanks," said Mike. "This will probably be the best biology report I've ever done!"

Dog barked again and looked stern.

"'Scuze me," said Mike, "the best biology report you've ever done? Oh, who cares? An A's an A. Right?"

Dog flipped up his screen to show Mike the report. "No, not here," said Mike. "Let's go back to my house and we'll load it on to my computer."

Mike and Dog took off down the street, but they did not see what lay ahead. Racing along at breakneck speed was none other than Stoat Muldoon: Alien Hunter, at the wheel of his hovervan.

"Well, Muldoon," said the alien hunter to himself, "you may not have sighted any aliens today, but you just keep on keepin' on. You have a duty to 'Protect the Planet,' so remember..." At that point, Muldoon reached down and pushed some buttons on the dashboard. The radio began to play Muldoon's theme song. Muldoon shook his head to the beat and joined in:

"Alien scum, they don't stand a chance.
They know who wears the pants.
Muldoooon!
He's the guy with all the right moves.
His website really grooves.
Muldoooon!
Not the man on the moon.
Just a man? No, Stoat Muldoon!
He's da man!
He's Stoat Muldoon!
He's da man!
He's Stoat Muldoon!
MULDOOOOON!"

Muldoon was busy singing along, when his gaze fell on Dog, who was flying along the sidewalk. Mike was across the street.

"Do my eyes deceive me?" said the alien

hunter, staring at Dog in disbelief.

Mike had recognized Muldoon's hovervan and knew Dog was in danger. "Dog! MOVE!" he yelled as he quickly hovered over to help Dog. But the hovervan was in his way.

Muldoon now caught sight of Mike. He tried to swerve, but it was too late, and Mike fell hard to the ground. Dog rushed over to help the boy as Muldoon screeched to a halt and got out of his hovervan.

Mike sat on the sidewalk, dazed and woozy from the fall. Then, before he could react, the alien hunter approached.

"Freeze, alien canine!" Muldoon commanded, pointing his Alien Tracking Device at Dog. He pressed a button and the MATD — Multipurpose Alien Tracking Device — fired a bright orange tractor beam that hit Dog, froze him, and levitated the robot off the ground. "You finally caught yourself a genuine alien," crowed Muldoon. But then he took a closer look at Dog and was not so certain. "Uh, at least, I think it's an alien..."

Mike's brain jerked quickly into gear. "No!" he cried. "Wait! Don't take him!"

"Sorry, son. It's my job," said Muldoon proudly as he loaded the frozen Dog into his hovervan. "But you can watch the alien dissection on my website, stoatmuldoon.com." Muldoon saluted Mike and was ready to leave.

"D-d-d-d-dissection..." stammered Mike. "OH, NO!"

WHAT'S HAPPENED TO DOG!

AFTER LEAVING MIKE stranded, Stoat Muldoon took Dog straight to Milicom 4, a top-secret government installation, somewhere in the desert. It was set up like the famous Area 51, and the head scientist, Dr. Brady Hacksaw, had an alien obsession to rival Muldoon's!

Once inside, Dog was taken to a laboratory and placed on a large round operating table. Muldoon now stood, looking him over, while the bald-headed Hacksaw worked at a console behind them. Two robot security guards were standing nearby. Hacksaw walked across to Dog, holding a laser-cutting device.

"Look at those big fiber-optic eyes," said Muldoon, staring affectionately at Dog, "begging me to take him home and give him a bowl of...whatever it is he eats. Hey fella, hey there, hey!"

Hacksaw looked irritated. "Excuse me, Muldoon," he said. "We're doing serious work here, not your cable show!"

"Sorry," said Muldoon. Then he added, "Oh, you've seen my show."

Hacksaw grimaced.

"Government lackey," spat Muldoon under his breath.

"I heard that," said the doctor as he activated the laser and moved toward Dog. "You'd better remember, Mr. Muldoon, you're only here because you brought this specimen in."

Not far away, hovering on their One Martian Air Bikes, or OMABs, the Butt-Uglies were using a tracking device to look for their robot companion. They veered down, out of the blue sky, and landed in the desert below. 2-T checked his wrist gauntlet and gestured at a point ahead of them.

All three Butt-Uglies got off their bikes and walked toward it.

"Okay, I've got him! Dog's signal is coming from over there," 2-T said.

As 2-T spoke, Mike, Angela, and Cedric glided in on their hoverboards.

"This isn't anywhere near Muldoon's place," said Mike.

"Maybe he decided to take Dog for a walk," suggested Cedric.

"Yeah, right, hello!" said Angela, rolling her eyes in disbelief. "He's a robot. He doesn't take walks!"

Then 2-T broke in, "He's here! My tracker says Dog's inside that rock."

"My brain says your tracker is screwy," said B.Bop.

Cedric walked over and examined the rock. "Guys," he said, knocking his fist on the large sandy object, "this rock is made of metal."

"Oh, maybe there's a trapdoor," said B.Bop sarcastically.

Cedric looked at the rock and shouted, "Open says me!"

B.Bop's jaw dropped and the others looked on in disbelief as the rock slid open and revealed a round opening with a ladder leading down a vertical tube.

"Well, I'll be a roasted Martian mud sucker," said B.Bop quietly.

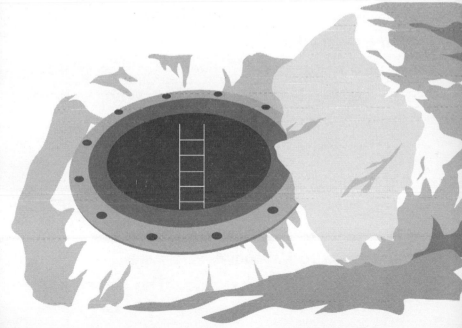

The Martians looked at one another. "I don't like secret entrances," said B.Bop suspiciously. "They're usually booby-trapped."

2-T agreed with him. "Yeah, there's never anything good behind a secret entrance. If there was, why would you need to hide it? Right?"

"That may be," said Do-Wah, looking worried, "but Dog's down there."

"He's right, 2-T," said B.Bop knowing, as the others did, that they had no choice but to go into the tube.

"Okay," said 2-T bravely, "let's go." Then he added less bravely, "Do-Wah, you're first."

The ladder led Do-Wah down the drain-like tube and to a hatch. Do-Wah heaved the hatch open and peered headfirst into an empty antechamber. It was the entrance to Milicom 4.

"Looks okay," he said. The room was

made entirely of metal. On one wall was a
door with a keypad. "Just a room with a
door at one end," Do-Wah added.

B.Bop gave the okay and he, 2-T, and the
kids climbed into the room. 2-T scanned
the door's keypad with his wrist gauntlet,
while Do-Wah continued to hang from the
ceiling hatch.

"Hatch lock," 2-T said matter-of-factly, looking at the keypad, "simple binary code. Hah, I could open this with my nose." Then he turned to Do-Wah. "You can quit hanging upside down now!" 2-T looked more closely at the keypad, then zapped it with a laser light from his wrist gauntlet. "Done!" he said triumphantly, and stepped back smiling.

But he had spoken too soon. A siren

immediately started wailing and with a loud *ka-chunk*, a larger steel door slid across the door 2-T had been working on. Another large door slid across the ceiling hatch, where they had all come in. Then, as the kids watched in horror, the back wall of the room began to slide inward. The steel chamber was about to crush everyone inside it!

"More like done FOR!" yelled B.Bop.

While the Butt-Uglies and the kids waited for their crushing end, Muldoon stood in Laboratory 01 of Milicom 4. The sliding doors in the antechamber had set off a siren in the laboratory, as well as flashing red warning lights.

Muldoon reacted to the siren and the lights as if he was being attacked by a band of crazed Calaban II mercenaries! He pulled out his MATD and prepared for battle.

"Well, dress me in ruffles and call me Sally!" he exclaimed. "Looks like we've got ourselves a little unauthorized alien activity."

Hacksaw, who was working on Dog, was altogether calmer. "I suggest you settle down," he said in a weary voice. "This is a secure, top-secret government facility."

Muldoon remained unconvinced. "Holy cow, man! What if it's the alien scalawag come to free its cherished pooch?"

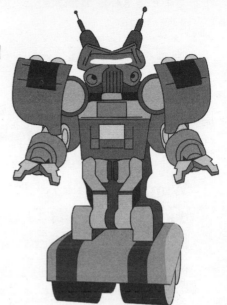

Hacksaw smiled cruelly. "Spare me your sentimentality, Muldoon. It's distracting. Besides, this place is guarded by the finest of government defense robots." He pointed to one of the robots that had trundled over to the lab door on its tank-type treads, then restarted his laser cutter.

Back in the antechamber, 2-T was working at fever pitch on the security keypad.

"Can you hurry up and stop this thing?" asked B.Bop urgently.

"Hey, it's not so easy," said 2-T. "I have all my best stuff loaded into Dog, okay?"

The walls were closing in fast. B.Bop, Do-Wah, and the kids pressed themselves against the walls to try to stop them, or at least to slow them down, but the effort was in vain.

As 2-T continued to work, B.Bop was running out of patience. "Right, that's it!" he said. "Time's up, Mr. Science — my turn." And with that, B.Bop leveled his wrist gauntlet at the keypad and blasted it to pieces.

There was a collective sigh of relief as the walls moved back

26

and the doors opened. 2-T looked half-elated, half-annoyed.

"Lucky shot," he snapped.

In Laboratory 01, the alarm lights had changed from red to blue, but Hacksaw was trying not to look ruffled. He handed a box to the robot security guard behind him and said, "Secure this."

"So, Mr. Government Employee," Stoat sneered, looking at the lights, "what does this change in the color scheme mean?"

At first, Hacksaw ignored him. Picking up an anti-alien device that looked just like Muldoon's, only smaller, he said, "It's just a code blue...intruders have breached the first level of security, but there's nothing to worry about."

Muldoon knew the smug scientist was

covering, and was enjoying seeing him on the defensive. "Aha!" he said. "You underestimated the alien mind?"

Hacksaw didn't answer. Instead he pressed some buttons on his MATD and left the laboratory. Muldoon held up his own MATD. "Yeah, well, mine's bigger than yours!" he crowed. Then he followed the scientist out of the laboratory.

Meanwhile, the Butt-Uglies and the kids had left the antechamber and were making their way along a catwalk. The scene that greeted them made the kids draw breath. They were in a huge cylindrical room, ringed and crossed with tubes, pipes, and catwalks. The catwalks connected to corridors, which in turn led to closed doors, while at the bottom of all this was a huge, churning turbine.

"Oh, maaaan!" exclaimed a stunned Mike. "This place is massive!"

"Okay," said B.Bop, "time to find Dog. 2-T, which way?"

2-T checked his wrist gauntlet tracking device. "That way," he said, pointing in one direction and heading off. Then he stopped as his tracker beeped. "And that way!" he said, pointing in the opposite direction. Two blips indicating Dog showed on his gauntlet's screen.

Do-Wah looked at 2-T in disbelief. "What are you talking about?" he said. "Dog can't be in two places at once!"

Angela gasped. "He can... if he's been..."

"Taken apart," said 2-T, putting into words what everyone was thinking. "And if it's true..."

"...Somebody's going to find out how it feels," interrupted B.Bop. "Two signals? We'd better split up..."

"Ooooooh! Nice choice of words, Shakespeare," said 2-T sarcastically.

"...And find Dog!" snapped B.Bop, finishing his sentence and not at all impressed with 2-T's joke.

B.Bop was about to divide the group, when Cedric put up his hand. "We've got company," he said as he pointed at three security robots, who were trundling along

on their tank tracks toward the group.

"Uh... oh!" cried Angela as the kids turned to make a run for it. But before they had a chance to get anywhere, two more robots, accompanied by Dr. Hacksaw, came into view at the other end of the catwalk. They were approaching fast.

Everyone turned and looked at B.Bop. After all, he was the leader!

"Here's the plan," said B.Bop quickly. "There is no plan!"

Suddenly, B.Bop leveled his wrist gauntlet at the catwalk ahead and blasted right through it. The part of the catwalk the Butt-Uglies and kids were standing on fell at a neat 45° angle toward a lower

level catwalk, making a perfect slide. B.Bop waited for everyone to slide down to the lower level, then blasted the top end of the slide away — leaving Hacksaw and the robots stranded above.

"Don't you think we should go and get them?" asked Muldoon, who had caught up with Hacksaw. He and the doctor looked down at the Butt-Uglies and the kids, who were running away below them.

Hacksaw turned to the alien hunter and scowled, "They won't get far." Then he snapped at the robot security guards, "Scour the lower levels!"

Meanwhile, the Butt-Uglies and the kids had run along the lower catwalk and were now faced with a "T" junction.

"Okay, we've got to split up here," said

2-T, not knowing which direction to take.

B.Bop pointed to the left corridor. "Do-Wah, you, Mike, and Cedric that way. Angela, you come with me and 2-T!"

"We meet at the OMABs in twenty!" said 2-T. "Don't keep us waiting!"

Do-Wah and the boys ran down their corridor and came to a closed door. Cedric pulled and pushed, but the door stayed shut. "It uh...won't open," he said as he continued to struggle.

"Yeah, sometimes you just have to jiggle it," said Do-Wah. Then the Martian smashed into the door with his head and shoulder. The entire thing snapped off its hinges and crashed to the floor! Do-Wah smiled. "Like that," he said.

Mike and Cedric were impressed.

"All right!" they yelled as they headed through the opening.

In another corridor, 2-T, B.Bop, and Angela had stopped, while 2-T used his gauntlet to get a better reading on Dog.

"He's just around the corner," said the tech commando.

But no one had a chance to follow 2-T. Instead they ducked, as a laser beam shot over their heads and blasted into the wall behind them.

"YEEOOW!" cried B.Bop.

Then he turned around and saw

a robot security guard getting too close for comfort.

B.Bop gestured to 2-T and Angela to run. "Go!" he said firmly. "I'll handle this guy." Angela and 2-T charged off down the corridor.

B.Bop, meanwhile, lowered his head like a bull and prepared to charge at the oncoming robot. "I saw this on the wrestling channel," he panted. "How hard can it be?"

Next thing, the Martian slammed headfirst into the robot's metal chest. The impact sent both the robot and B.Bop crashing backward.

"Ooooh! That hurt!" whimpered B.Bop. He looked up and saw electric sparks shooting from the robot. "Now, that is shocking behavior!" he laughed, jumping to his feet and dusting himself off.

A whining noise was now coming from the

battered security guard. B.Bop decided he needed to get away before the robot did something electronically unpleasant to itself. But, as he turned and ran, he was thrown to the ground by a powerful explosion. The robot had self-destructed and bits of it flew everywhere.

"That never happened in wrestling," said the plucky Martian, getting up and heading back along the corridor.

Before long he came to a door marked "Lab 01." He opened it and went in. Angela and 2-T were already there. B.Bop looked at the operating table in front of them. "Hey, you found Dog?" he said, breathing heavily after his bout with the robot.

"Well, yes...and no," 2-T said.

B.Bop came closer to the table. "What does that mean?" he asked.

2-T stepped to one side and B.Bop took a closer look.

All he could see was Dog's head!

"AW, MAN!" he cried.

As this was happening in Lab 01, Mike, Cedric, and Do-Wah had found themselves in nearby Lab 02. In this laboratory, there was a long row of large glass holding cells for specimens or prisoners.

"This place just gets worse," said Mike.

"It's like a dog pound — but for aliens," Cedric added.

Suddenly, Do-Wah motioned for them to be quiet. "Get down. Someone's coming," he whispered loudly.

Cedric and Mike ducked down, while Do-Wah stood beside the door. When the door flew open, he was hidden behind it.

Two robot security guards rolled in. One was carrying the box Dr. Hacksaw had given it earlier. The robot made its way over to a glass cell, opened it, and locked the box inside. Then the two security robots glided out of the laboratory.

As the door closed behind the guards, Do-Wah's wrist gauntlet began to beep wildly. "Oh, grix!" exclaimed Do-Wah. "I'm getting a signal from the box."

He and the boys walked over to the glass cell where the robot had put the box. Cedric then pressed a button that opened the cell's door, just as he'd seen the security guard do. Do-Wah pulled out the box.

At first, both he and the boys were hesitant to open it. What could be inside? Then they sighed and made the decision. Do-Wah carefully opened the box.

Inside, to their disgust, they saw Dog's body — HEADLESS!

"Poor Dog," said Do-Wah wretchedly, "what'd they do to you?"

"The same thing I'm going to do to you," said a voice from the other side of the room, "if you don't surrender."

Mike, Cedric, and Do-Wah looked up to see the dreaded Dr. Hacksaw, accompanied by two of his robots. There was no escape. Do-Wah and the boys were well and truly cornered. There was only one thing they could do. They raised their hands in the air and gave themselves up.

3

WATCH OUT! THERE'S A NITCHUP ABOUT!

HACKSAW ORDERED HIS robots to place Do-Wah, Mike, and Cedric in three glass cells. Cedric's was at the end of the row, near a cell that contained a small, gray, cute-looking alien creature.

Cedric looked at it. "What'd they get you on buddy?" he asked in his best prison-type lingo. "We're here for saving a mechanical Martian Dog!"

The Nitchup made a purring sound.

"That's a Nitchup," said Do-Wah, surprised to see this alien on Earth. "Nicest guys in the galaxy — real sensitive. I can't believe anyone would want to put a Nitchup in a cage."

A little later, Stoat Muldoon came into the lab where Do-Wah, Mike, and Cedric were imprisoned. He was carrying the box that contained Dog's body. "Well, I hope you've learned your lesson, youngsters," he said. "Infiltrating top government installations with alien invaders has landed you right in the hoosegow."

"Would it help if we said we were sorry?" Mike asked, with a hint of sarcasm.

"It never hurts," said Muldoon as he put Dog's box down on a table where Mike had left his Butt-Ugly Martian communicator. At that moment, Hacksaw walked in.

"Okay, keep the aliens," said Muldoon to Hacksaw, "but I think these youngsters can be set free now." Then he chuckled. "Unless you're planning on opening them up, too!"

Hacksaw turned to Muldoon and stared. He wanted no nonsense. This lab was deadly serious to him. "The kids stay. They have breached the security of our top-secret installation. Nobody knows we're here and I plan to keep it that way."

Suddenly, a noise came from the table. It was Mike's communicator. The device crackled and beeped, then a voice said, "Hey, Mike, we've got Dog's head. How are you guys doing?"

Muldoon wasted no time in picking up the communicator. "Who's there?" he said. "Identify yourselves."

Inside Laboratory 01, B.Bop looked at 2-T in surprise. "Oh, oh!" he said. "It's Muldoon. Get a lock on that communicator." Then he spoke into his device. "Welcome to Quantum Burgers. Can I interest you in our special — Alien Hunter

Nutcase Burger? It comes with a special toy surprise..."

Muldoon wasn't impressed. "You think this is some kind of joke?" he replied.

But B.Bop was ready to go and turned to 2-T in anticipation. 2-T looked at his wrist gauntlet and punched in a calculation. "Down the hall, two doors to the left," he said.

"Let's bust them out!" said B.Bop heroically, and the two Martians rushed out of Lab 02, ready for business. Angela picked up Dog's head and followed. "I've got Dog," she said weakly, "kind of..."

Inside Laboratory 02, Muldoon was standing beside the door, still worrying about the fate of the kids, and about to lose his temper, big time. "Secret lab or not," he said sternly, "those young men are citizens of Earth, card-carrying members of the human race, and should be..."

But before Muldoon could finish his sentence, the door to the lab crashed open, squashing the hapless alien hunter behind it. B.Bop and 2-T stood in the doorway.

The Martians raised their wrist gauntlets and scanned the room, while Angela stood behind them.

"FROZE!" cried B.Bop.

"That's freeze, guys," said Angela as she pushed past. "He's a foreigner," she added, explaining B.Bop's mistake to Hacksaw and Muldoon.

Hacksaw stood beside a table. Near his hand was a small anti-alien device. "Well, it's the alien cavalry," he sneered. "How quaint." Quickly, Hacksaw snatched up the device. "Now, back off..." he said, pointing

it at Do-Wah, "...or little butt-ugly over there is going to be little butt toast."

B.Bop reacted swiftly. He dived and rolled, distracting the doctor, and then, with his wrist gauntlet laser, shot the anti-alien device straight out of Hacksaw's hand!

"WOOOOH! Bust a move!" yelled Cedric.

Then he and Mike began to chant, "Go B.Bop! Go B.Bop!"

2-T and B.Bop grabbed Hacksaw and held his hands behind his back. "You won't

get away with this," said the government man angrily.

"We just did, babe!" said 2-T.

Quickly, the Butt-Uglies removed the kids from their cells and placed Hacksaw in one of his own. Do-Wah smiled and said lovingly, "If I had more time, I'd put newspaper down. Sorry."

B.Bop, meanwhile, was standing guard at the door. He looked over his shoulder and asked, "Any progress with Dog?"

Angela was helping 2-T to pop Dog's head onto his body. Once his head was back on, Dog sprang to life and placed his front paws on 2-T's chest. Then he barked gleefully, glad to be operational again.

"He's as good as the day I built him," said the tech commando. "Hey, did you check out the Nitchup?"

B.Bop looked at the creature. "Didn't think a Nitchup would come anywhere near

Earth — they're so sensitive." Then he jerked a thumb toward the door. It was time to go.

"Yeah," said 2-T, "let's blow this place before we're all specimens."

On his way out, B.Bop pulled the door to close it, and the forgotten Muldoon fell onto the floor — still unconscious. B.Bop looked down. "I guess the excitement got to him," he said.

Meanwhile, Cedric had edged over to the Nitchup's cell. He hated to see the little fellow caged. The Nitchup pressed his face against the glass. He looked so cute and appealing. "Don't worry, little guy," said Cedric as he hit the lock release button to the cell. "I won't leave you stuck in here."

The door to the glass cell slowly lifted up and the little Nitchup was gradually exposed to the Earth's air. As this

happened, the cute-looking alien creature began to glow red. But Cedric did not see the change take place. He had already rushed off on the trail of Angela, Mike, Dog, and the Butt-Uglies.

The gang were soon speeding down the corridor. But as they turned a corner, they stopped cold!

Three robot security guards blocked their way, looking like a set of bowling pins. Each was equipped with laser fire epaulets, which they activated as soon as they saw the enemy in front of them.

Luckily B.Bop had the answer. "POWER BALL, NOW!" he yelled.

All three Martians fired their wrist gauntlet beams toward the robots — but slightly off target. The power streams shot out, then came together to form a huge power ball, which screamed toward the security guards. The power ball engulfed the robots and exploded.

When the smoke cleared, the three robot guards were smashed to pieces.

It was a great hit and the kids jumped up and down with glee.

"STRIIIIIIKE!" yelled Mike.

"Very cool!" added Cedric.

Meanwhile, back in Lab 02, Stoat Muldoon was just coming round. His brain was still feeling woolly and he held his head in his hands. "Note to file," he said woozily. "Where am I?" Then he started, as he heard a voice coming from somewhere in the room.

"Muldoon, hurry!" yelled the voice. "Let me out of here. The aliens have escaped and we've got to capture them!"

Muldoon slowly realized where he was. His first clear thoughts, though, were for the kids. "And...what about the youngsters?" he enquired.

Inside the cell, Hacksaw threw up his hands in resignation. Muldoon had the upper hand. "Okay! Okay! They can go!" he screamed. "Just get me out of here!"

Muldoon was beginning to enjoy the situation. "Say 'Pretty please, Mr. Muldoon: Alien Hunter.'"

Hacksaw stared at Muldoon with a look of pure hatred on his face.

In the clear desert air, away from Muldoon and Hacksaw, a large domelike rock began to move. The rock slid across the sand and the kids, the Butt-Ugly Martians, and an intact, fully-functional Dog climbed out of the round hatch. At last, everyone was free.

"We made it!" said Mike, relieved. "I think the OMABs and the hoverboards are just over there."

Angela followed Mike and the others as they walked toward their machines. "Thanks for saving us, 2-T," she said.

Cedric looked at her, then at the Martians. "I did my bit, too," he said matter-of-factly.

"Oh, yeah?" said 2-T, wondering what Cedric was talking about.

"Uh huh. I let that cute little Nitchup guy out of his cell," continued Cedric.

Cedric might as well have said that Emperor Bog had landed with a hoard of Martians. All three Butt-Uglies froze on the spot.

"You...let...it...OUT?" gasped B.Bop, hardly able to say the words.

Angela and Mike looked at Cedric. Slowly Angela asked, "Why do I think that wasn't a good thing?"

"I felt sorry for it," said Cedric. "You guys said it was a sensitive creature."

B.Bop gave Cedric a look of despair, and explained, "It is sensitive — sensitive to EARTH'S ATMOSPHERE!"

"If a Nitchup is exposed to Earth's atmosphere," explained 2-T, "its blood hydrogenates. It'll reach critical mass in a matter of hours!"

Mike was almost afraid to ask the next question. "What happens then?"

"Nothing..." said B.Bop, "that is, as long

as you're at least a hundred thousand miles away. Otherwise, let's just say, you'd better get out the marshmallows!"

"Other than that, they are real nice guys," added Do-Wah.

Mike was in a hurry to get going now.

"The OMABs are this way," he said.

The Butt-Uglies were looking in the other direction at the installation's rock door.

"Yeah," said B.Bop, "but the Nitchup is THIS way. And we either get it off this planet before it reaches critical mass, or there isn't gonna be a planet!"

With that, the Butt-Uglies returned to the secret entrance, and climbed back down the ladder and into Milicom 4. Mike, Angela, and Cedric watched as the Martians disappeared once more into the secret government installation.

Inside, the Butt-Uglies reopened the door that led out of the antechamber. This time they managed not to set off any alarms, but they were still in for a shock. When the door opened, Dr. Brady Hacksaw, Stoat Muldoon, and a gaggle of security robots were waiting for them.

All the three Butt-Ugly Martians could do was to raise their arms and give themselves up.

"Smile and say 'We surrender,'" advised 2-T.

WHO'S GOT
THE NITCHUP?

4

INSIDE LAB 01, things were not looking good for the Martians. All three were now strapped to the large round operating table. Muldoon watched wide-eyed as Hacksaw lowered his laser-cutting instruments toward 2-T. The excitement was making the doctor drool.

"Dissection..." said the overexcited

Hacksaw, sounding a bit too much like Emperor Bog's henchman, the evil Dr. Damage, "...dissection's good."

"I know he reminds me of someone," said B.Bop. "It's gonna come to me."

2-T looked disgusted. "You know, I never thought the last thing I'd see would be some guy's drool!"

"Hey, Muldoon!" B.Bop yelled. "We gave ourselves up. Aren't you afraid it's a trick?"

Muldoon put up his hand to stall Hacksaw. "Wait, alien trickery! Could it be? I think not. Let's go!" Then he thought of his TV show. "But wait — this could make my season premiere a real ratings grabber. Do you guys have a video camera around here?"

In the desert outside Milicom 4, Mike was trying to contact the Martians on his communicator, but he was getting no response. He knew that they must be in trouble and he was determined to help. He looked around for the rock that led to the government installation. "We've got to rescue the Martians!" he said bravely. Then he remembered the password that had opened the rock before and shouted, "Open says me!"

But the rock didn't do a thing.

Cedric joined him and tried again. "Open, says me!"

"Hello, guys," Angela called, "I think you're at the wrong rock!" She indicated another rock near her that was opening. "Maybe I should lead," she added coolly.

Back in Lab 01, Hacksaw was becoming impatient with Muldoon and his antics.

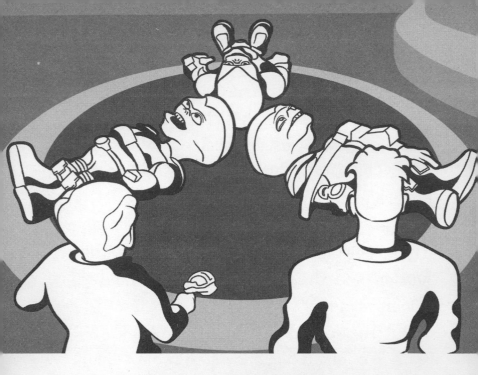

The Butt-Uglies watched as he raised his dissecting gear and threatened Muldoon with it.

"Sixty seconds, Muldoon," he spat, "then I start dissecting!"

Muldoon looked at Hacksaw, then at 2-T. "All right, give me one good reason why I shouldn't have the scientist here open you up," he said.

2-T looked up at the alien hunter and

said mysteriously, "Because one of our internal organs is filled with a poison gas that will kill you on contact."

"Really?" said Do-Wah. "Which one?"

Muldoon rolled his eyes. "Note to file. Martians are lousy liars."

Hacksaw's sixty seconds were now up. He swiveled his laser blades like a pair of Colt .45s and approached the operating table. "Let's see what you're made of, boys," he grinned.

2-T looked at him wide-eyed. "Phew. This guy needs some serious therapy!"

Meanwhile, unknown to Hacksaw and Muldoon, the Nitchup was free and racing down one of the installation corridors.

Before long, the little creature came upon a security robot. The robot ran after him and quickly announced the alien's escape across the building's loud speaker systems: "Security alert! Specimen Q974 has breached containment."

Back in Lab 01, Hacksaw heard the alarming announcement just in time to stop him from dissecting 2-T. The doctor ran out of the room shouting to his guards, "The Nitchup has escaped. Shoot him. Vaporize him. TAKE HIM OUT!"

"Stay right there," said Muldoon to the Martians as he followed Hacksaw. "Stoat Muldoon: Alien Hunter will be right back."

"What?" said 2-T. "Are you going to show a commercial before you dissect us?"

Muldoon threw up his arms in irritation, and headed after Hacksaw.

"I'll take that as a no," said 2-T.

Meanwhile, the kids and Dog were looking for the Martians when they spotted the Nitchup. The cute-looking creature was running along, trying to get away from the security robot. The kids and Dog headed after them.

In Lab 01, the Martians were still lying strapped to the dissecting table. But now everything was strangely quiet.

"If we don't break out of these restraints," said B.Bop, "that nut is gonna come back. And it's gonna hurt — a lot."

"A lot, a lot," added Do-Wah.

"Do-Wah, you're stronger than me and B.Bop put together. Can't you break free?" asked 2-T.

"I don't know," said Do-Wah.

B.Bop wasn't impressed. "What do you mean 'I don't know'?" he asked. He couldn't believe that Do-Wah could be this stupid.

"Well, I didn't really try. I thought this was part of your plan," replied Do-Wah weakly.

B.Bop and 2-T sighed in disbelief.

Outside Lab 01, the kids had lost the Nitchup and were looking for the Martians.

"Well, there's no sign of them," said Mike to the others.

Just then, the door ahead flew off its hinges and crashed against the opposite wall. The flying door was followed by the Butt-Uglies, who had finally broken free!

"Let me revise that," said Mike. "I think I know where they are." Then he turned to his Martian friends. "Are we glad to see you guys."

"Likewise, I'm sure," replied 2-T.

"All right, look," said B.Bop to the kids, "you guys take Dog and get out of here as fast as you can! 2-T, Do-Wah, we're gonna play Nitchup, Nitchup, who's got the Nitchup?"

Hacksaw wasted no time in catching up with the Nitchup. The poor creature was now cowering against a corridor wall as the Doctor and Muldoon loomed over it with MATDs in hand. Muldoon, however, was not so sure.

"Do you really have to destroy it?" he asked Hacksaw.

Hacksaw looked at him, "Don't go weak on me, Muldoon," he sneered.

"Well, at least let me get a photo first, for my website," answered the alien hunter, pressing some buttons on his tracking device. Muldoon pointed his

MATD at the Nitchup to take the photo. The creature's image came up on the device's screen. The Nitchup looked far too cute to harm.

"Stand back, you imbecile!" shouted Dr. Hacksaw, untouched by Muldoon's pathetic sentiments.

"This isn't right," persisted Muldoon. "He's just a poor little defenseless alien creature. He couldn't hurt anyone."

Still the doctor wasn't moved. He lifted his MATD, ready to fire at the alien, but as he did so, a short, sharp order rang out behind him.

"STOP!"

Muldoon and Hacksaw turned around to where the order had come from. B.Bop, 2-T, and Do-Wah stood before them.

"If you shoot that alien," continued B.Bop, "it'll explode and take this planet — and maybe one or two more with it!"

"You don't really expect me to fall for that," scowled Hacksaw. "Besides, who's going to stop me?" The doctor motioned toward gangs of robot security guards, who stood menacingly at each end of the corridor.

"Uh...well, we are," said B.Bop.

"It's what we do," said Do-Wah.

Then B.Bop began the Butt-Ugly Martians' transformation chant: "B!" he shouted.

"K!" cried 2-T.

"M!" yelled Do-Wah. And the Martians changed into full B.K.M. Instantly, they were equipped with the most powerful of weapons. When their transformation was complete, they shouted their battle cry, "LET'S GET UGLY!"

"Get them. Shoot them. VAPORIZE THEM!" screamed Hacksaw. But it was too late. The Martians were about to make light work of his security robots.

First 2-T launched himself at three robots at one end of the corridor, knocking them over like tenpins.

Then B.Bop spun and spiraled into the robots at the other end of the corridor, leaving them in pieces.

"And the Martians pick up the difficult seven-ten split!" joked 2-T.

Now Do-Wah flew like lightning, his head lowered and aimed at the wall, where the Nitchup was standing. But, at the very last moment, he veered away from the wall and grabbed the Nitchup. "I've got the little guy," he called.

"I've got the big ones!" yelled back B.Bop as he rammed more security robots on the way down the corridor. The three

Butt-Ugly Martians were now heading out.

Hacksaw was frantic. "Those ugly aliens are getting away!" he stormed.

"And they're taking the cute little one with them," said Muldoon, more than a little relieved.

Minutes later, the Butt-Uglies had made their way, with the Nitchup, out of Milicom 4, to where the kids were waiting.

"You guys take Nitchup and meet us at ZAPZ," said B.Bop.

Mike grabbed the cute little alien and hopped on his hoverboard. Then he, Angela, and Cedric sped back over the desert toward the city and ZAPZ.

"Okay, boys," said B.Bop as the kids headed out of view, "it's time to build us a sand castle."

"Roger that, Commander," said 2-T and Do-Wah.

The Butt-Uglies flew off until they were about fifty meters from the dome-rock entrance. Then they landed on the desert ground. They each fired their lasers furiously into the sand, pushing up a huge mountain of dirt over the entrance rock of

Milicom 4. Soon it was completely covered.

"There, that ought to hold them for a while," said Do-Wah.

2-T agreed, "Yeah, now let's get back to ZAPZ," he added urgently.

At ZAPZ, the kids and the Martians stood in front of the Nitchup. B.Bop knew they were running out of time.

"We have to get this little guy out of this atmosphere right away," he said. "Some place where he can't hurt anyone." Then he paused and added meaningfully, "At least, anyone we care about."

"Wait, you're not thinking what I'm thinking," said 2-T with a twinkle in his eye.

"I'm not?" said B.Bop.

THE BIG BANG THEORY

"You wouldn't?" smiled 2-T.

Do-Wah grinned, "Oh, yes he would!"

"We have to." B.Bop laughed.

The kids looked from one Martian to the other. They were getting confused.

"What are you guys talking about?" demanded Angela.

Cedric looked even more confused, "They're not even speaking Martian and I still don't understand them."

Quickly, the Butt-Uglies made their way to their transmission panel. B.Bop called up Dr. Damage on board the *Bogstar*. "You know how you're always sending us stuff?" he said good-naturedly. "Well, we thought we'd send you something 'special' — just for you. We know you'll have a blast!"

"Really!" said the delighted Damage. "Maybe I misjudged you three. Oh, goody! Here it comes." Then he let out a blood-curdling scream. "AAAAAAH! A Nitchup!

Emperor Bog!" he yelled. But at that moment, the screen crackled with static and the image of Damage disappeared.

"Did you guys just blow up the *Bogstar*?" asked Mike in disbelief.

"Nah," said B.Bop. "They probably got him out of there just in time."

"But we can dream, can't we," said 2-T as the Butt-Uglies high-fived.

The next day, Mike was at home, talking to the Butt-Uglies on his TV phone console.

"Come on, Mike," said B.Bop, "we're having a virtual reality tournament of champions. It won't be the same without you."

"I told you," said Mike. "I've gotta finish my report." Then Mike's mom called out that his dinner was ready. "I can't, Mom," Mike said. "I've gotta finish my report."

"Uh... I thought you said you'd finished that report," said Mike's mom.

"Um, well, I did, sort of, but... ah... well... Dog ate it."

"Oh," replied Mike's mom, "that's too bad... Mike?"

"Yes Mom."

"We don't have a dog?"

Mike rolled his eyes at his stupidity. The Martians were still there... laughing...

DON'T MISS THE NEXT EXCITING BUTT-UGLY ADVENTURE
MEET GORGON

Emperor Bog has sent the Butt-Uglies a brand-new weapon: Dr. Damage's Molecular De-atomizer. Unfortunately, a weapons-thieving, shape-shifting alien named Gorgon has stolen it — and captured the Butt-Uglies! Can the Butt-Uglies break free and finish off the evil alien? Or have they finally run out of luck?

Join the adventure and help the Martians save Earth! **LET'S GET UGLY!**